...an the **EVIL**

SI...LIES be defeated?

'My class absolutely **LOVED** it!'

REBECCA AND YEAR THREE AT
ST BARNABAS SCHOOL

Prepare for the
**SLIMIEST
ADVENTURE** ever!

The **FUNNIEST**
bunch of **GOO** in the

OXFORD
UNIVERSITY PRESS

Great Clarendon Street, Oxford OX2 6DP

Oxford University Press is a department of the University of Oxford.
It furthers the University's objective of excellence in research, scholarship,
and education by publishing worldwide. Oxford is a registered trade mark
of Oxford University Press in the UK and in certain other countries

Database right Oxford University Press (maker)

First published 2018

British Library Cataloguing in Publication Data

Data available

ISBN: 978-0-19-276376-1

1 3 5 7 9 10 8 6 4 2

Printed in China

WELCOME TO THE
WORLD OF
SLIME

SIX *AWESOME* LEVELS TO EXPLORE

Enter a team into the great **GUNGE GAMES**. There are loads of slimy sports to take part in, and win!

Leap from platform to platform, to reach the dizzying heights of the **CRUSTY CRATER**. Whatever you do, don't look down.

It's a dash to the finish line as you speed around this ultimate racing circuit. Can you reach **SLIME CENTRAL** in one piece?

Battle it out in a mission to capture the **FUNGUS FORT**. Beware: you'll need more than ninja skills to defeat the enemies on this level.

Can you escape from the **MONSTROUS MAZE**? Just when you think you're on the right track, the ghostly Gools will be ready to attack.

Dare you enter the dungeon of slime? Watch your step or you just might end up stuck in the **BOG OF BEASTS**!

THE STORY SO FAR

After accidentally **sneezing** all over his tablet computer, Max found himself whisked inside his favourite app, **WORLD OF SLIME**, where he came face-to-face with the Goozillas, a group of green, **slimy** creatures he had created in the game.

When Max discovered that his **sneeze** had destroyed the **GOLDEN GLOB**—a magical artefact that keeps the **WORLD OF SLIME** goo flowing—and that without it the Goozillas' volcano home would completely dry out, he teamed up with his icky new

friends and set off to
retrieve all the missing pieces,
hoping to fix the **GOLDEN GLOB**
and bring back the **Slime**.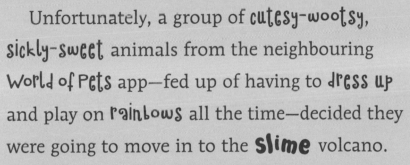

Unfortunately, a group of cutesy-wootsy,
sickly-sweet animals from the neighbouring
World of Pets app—fed up of having to dress up
and play on rainbows all the time—decided they
were going to move in to the **Slime** volcano.

If the evil Bubble Kitten and her band of
Sicklies get the **GOLDEN GLOB** pieces, then it's
the end for the Goozillas, and so thanks to that
one fateful **Sneeze**, Max has found himself in
a frantic race not just to save his new friends,
but all of **WORLD OF SLIME** itself!

MEET THE GOOZILLAS

JOE

The joker of the gang. Equipped with special slime-seeking gadget glasses.

GLOOP

The first Goozilla that Max created, and his favourite by far.

ATISHOO

A teeny, baby Goozilla, with an enormous sneeze.

GUNK

A mean, green, fighting machine!

BIG BLOB

Supersized, and super strong, but definitely not super smart.

CAPTAIN CRUST

Old, crusty, and in command.

and the sicklies

BUBBLE KITTEN

The evil leader of the Sicklies. She can blow bubble kisses to trap her enemies.

SUGAR PAWS PUPPY

Bubble Kitten's faithful sidekick. His sticky puw prints will stop you in your tracks.

GLITTER CHICK

Watch out for her eggs-plosive glitterbomb eggs.

DREAMY BUNNY

Beware of her powerful hypnotic gaze.

SQUEAKY GUINEA PIG

His supersonic screech will leave your ears ringing.

SCAMPY HAMSTER

The ultimate kickass, streel-fighting, rodent.

CHAPTER ONE

SNEEZE, PLEASE

Max slipped back under his covers, listened to make sure no one had heard him moving around, then switched on the tablet. It let out a **BLAST** of music as it powered on, and he quickly stuffed it under his pillow to silence it.

Holding his breath, Max listened again. It was six o'clock in the morning, and everyone else in the house was fast asleep. If his parents caught him playing on the tablet before breakfast, he'd be in trouble. Luckily, he could still hear his dad snoring like a **CHAINSAW** in the room next door, and if

Mum could sleep through that, she could sleep through anything.

Max yawned and waited for the tablet to finish loading. He was tired, but too **EXCITED** to sleep. Ever since he'd discovered he could sneeze himself inside his favourite app, he'd been able to think about very little else.

He'd already had two adventures with the game's characters, the Goozillas, but there was lots more fun to be had. Besides, the evil—yet completely adorable—Bubble Kitten and her sidekick, Sugar Paws Puppy, may have been defeated last time, but he knew they'd be back, and the Goozillas might just need his help. Being in the game was fun, but keeping the Goozillas and their home safe was much more important.

The tablet finished loading, and Max tapped the **WORLD OF SLIME** icon. After a quick loading screen, he was presented with the **slime** volcano that made up the world. The bottom level, where the Goozillas usually hung around, was completely empty.

Well, no. That wasn't quite true. Some of the half-finished Goozillas he'd created were milling around the place, bumping into walls and falling over each other. Physically, they all looked pretty much identical, and

Max hadn't bothered to give them any sort of personality. His friends, though—the Goozillas he'd devoted more time to creating back when he'd first got the app—were nowhere to be seen.

Max pulled the covers over his head and studied the screen. 'That's weird. Where are they?' he whispered.

He scrolled up to the volcano's second level, the **MONSTROUS MAZE**. He and his friends had recently been trapped there, and he worried for a moment that they might have wandered back in and got themselves lost.

But nope. Other than a few ghosts *ROAMING* around the maze, there was nobody there.

Max scrolled up to the next floor. Level three was a war game, complete with fighter drones, missile towers, and an **ENORMOUS** fort. He didn't actually play that level very often, because some of the enemies were far too hard to defeat.

At first, everything seemed normal enough on the level. Max was about to scroll away when he spotted a familiar monster truck-sized vehicle with **ENORMOUS** caterpillar tracks where its wheels should have been.

'The Bogey Bus!' Max said, then he clamped a hand over

his mouth. 'What's that doing there?' he whispered.

Pinching and zooming, Max spotted six blobs of various shapes and sizes cowering behind the bus as a fleet of flying drones **SWOOPED** towards them. It was the Goozillas. And they were in trouble!

'I'm coming, guys!' Max said. He held the tablet right in front of his face and twitched his nose. He just had to **sneeze** on the screen, and he'd be transported straight to the Goozillas' side.

'That's all. Just one **sneeze**,' he whispered, sniffing and wriggling his nose again.

The problem was, he hadn't **sneezed** since yesterday afternoon. The cold that had turned his head into a **snot-factory** had mostly cleared up now, and no matter how hard he concentrated, no **sneezes** were coming.

'**A . . . A . . .**' He tried faking it in the hope a real **sneeze** snuck in and finished the job, but no such luck. The Goozillas were in danger, and there was nothing he could do to help them.

Or was there . . . ?

Scrambling out from beneath his covers, Max pulled his pillow out of its case and ran a hand across its surface. Something sharp pricked against his palm, and he quickly trapped it between finger and thumb. With a **YANK**, he pulled out a single white feather.

Burrowing under his covers again, Max tickled his left nostril with the feather. Almost immediately, his eyes began to water.

He tickled the right nostril. His nose twitched all on its own. 'Come on,' Max urged, wriggling the feather right up inside his nose.

That did it! Max grabbed the tablet and held it in front of his face just as his head flew forward and a spray of snot splattered the screen.

ATCHOO!

The same feeling as before rolled over him, like the world was turning upside-down, inside-out, and back to front all at the same time.

'**YES!**' cried Max, as he was transported from his bed into the **WORLD OF SLIME**.

But his celebration was short-lived. Max was back in the **WORLD OF SLIME**, standing right next to the Bogey Bus. That was the good news. The bad news was, he was also in the path of a flying drone with a large gun attached to it.

And it was closing in fast!

CHAPTER TWO

THE DRONE ZONE

The drone's engine **WHIRRED** as it *SLICED* through the sky towards Max. It was an oval of shiny silver, with helicopter-like blades fixed to each of its arms.

Attached to the bottom of the drone was a miniature cannon. It opened fire, spraying the ground with a hail of golf ball-sized pellets. Max watched in amazement as the rock cracked and split where each pellet hit it.

Then, right before Max suffered the same fate, a blobby green shape barged into him, knocking him to safety. The drone's pellets *SLAMMED* into the side of the Bogey Bus, then the little flying vehicle banked sharply and flew away.

'Phew! That was close!' said Gloop. He had always been Max's favourite Goozilla, but Max liked him even more now. He'd just saved his life, after all. 'Now come on, before it comes back!'

Gloop rolled upright, and grabbed Max by the hand. '**WHAT'S GOING ON?**' Max yelped, as the Goozilla dragged him around to the other side of the Bogey Bus.

'Explain later,' said Gloop. 'Hide now!'

As Max stumbled around the Bogey Bus, he found the other Goozillas, all taking cover. The gun-toting Gunk and the dry-and-crunchy Captain Crust both swung their weapons towards him, and Max threw

up his hands in surrender.

'Wait! It's just me!' he said, then he
threw himself to the ground as another rain
of pellets R**A**T**T**L**E**D against the Bogey Bus
like the world's fastest drum solo. Several of

the bus's windows **SHATTERED**, showering the inside with glass. 'What's going on?' he yelped.

'Bubble Kitten came back while you were gone,' explained Joe, removing his Gadget Glasses and cleaning them on his slimy belly. When he put them back on, they were even dirtier than they had been. 'She's got the third piece of the **GOLDEN GLOB**.'

 Max **GASPED**. The Goozillas needed all six parts of the **GOLDEN GLOB** to bring the **slime** back to their volcano. Without the **slime** the whole place would eventually dry out—the Goozillas included. Bubble Kitten was determined to keep the **slime** from returning so she and her Sicklies could escape World of Pets and live in the volcano instead.

'Someone thought we could get it ourselves without your help,' said Atishoo, the smallest of Max's flubbery friends. He was sitting on Captain Crust's hat, and shot Gunk an accusing look.

'**THIS AIN'T MY FAULT, BUB**,' Gunk growled. 'How was I supposed to know she'd figure out how to use the flying . . . things?'

'Precisely the point,' sniffed Captain Crust, his moustache twitching angrily.

'You had no idea what we were walking into. You just rushed in without thinking—as usual!'

Gunk shrugged. 'Hey, things ain't that bad.'

More pellets peppered the side of the Bogey Bus, **DENTING** the metal and **SHATTERING** another of the windows.

'OK, they're pretty bad,' Gunk admitted.

Big Blob, the largest of the Goozillas, peered at Max for a moment, blinking slowly. After what felt like a long time, his face broke into a gummy smile. '**HEY, LOOK! MAX IS HERE**,' he announced.

'Hi, Blob,' said Max, waving to the big guy. Big Blob was the strongest Goozilla ever, but all those strength points meant there hadn't been any left over for brainpower.

Gloop and Joe both peeked around the side of the Bogey Bus. The drone was banking around again, getting ready for another attack. 'It's coming back,' Joe whispered. 'What are we going to do?'

Max thought for a moment. He was about to suggest a plan when Gunk threw himself against the side of the Bogey Bus and began clambering towards the roof.

'LEAVE IT TO ME,' Gunk announced.

'I'M TAKING THIS THING DOWN!'

Pulling himself onto the top of the bus, Gunk ran to the edge then threw himself towards the oncoming drone.

The drone dodged sharply left. Gunk's eyes went wide and he frantically flapped his stubby arms. A second later, he hit the ground with a damp **SPLAT**.

Captain Crust tutted beneath his moustache. 'Rushing in, as usual,' he muttered.

'Can't you just shoot it down?' asked Max.

'Negative,' said the captain. 'We've tried. The blasted thing's **INDESTRUCTIBLE**.'

Max shook his head. 'No, it's not. I've played this level and beaten the drones before. They've got a weakness.'

'Great!' Gloop cheered. 'What is it?'

Max frowned. 'Um . . . I can't remember.'

'Joe, your Gadget Glasses!' Max cried. 'Can you scan the drone and find its weak point?'

'I can try,' said Joe.

Ducking around the side of the bus, Joe

searched the sky for
the drone. He saw it as
it curved smoothly in a
semi-circle, then lined
itself up for another attack run.

'Scanning now,' he announced, tapping
a tiny button on the side of his frames. The
lenses of his glasses lit up red. 'There! In
that trench in the bottom! There's a reset
button. One hit should do it.'

'Great work!' Max cheered. He turned to
Captain Crust. 'Gunk's still down, so it's up
to you, Captain. Use your *SNOTSHOOTER*
to take that thing out.'

Captain Crust looked at the cane in his
hands. It was one of the most basic weapons
in the game, and nowhere near as powerful

as Gunk's *SLUDGESPUTTER 6000* gun. The lack of firepower wasn't the problem, though.

'I'm afraid my hands aren't as steady as they used to be, young Max,' he said. He held the cane out to Max. 'Perhaps you should do the honours this time?'

Max felt his heart speed up as he took the cane. He'd never fired one before, much less shot at a moving target.

'Uh, guys!' Gunk cried from down on the ground. 'It's coming back.'

'Here, Max, use these!' said Joe. He whipped off his Gadget Glasses and tossed them to Max, just as Max raced around the side of the Bogey Bus.

The drone was *SPEEDING* towards the

fallen Gunk, its cannon taking aim. There was no time to lose!

Balancing Joe's glasses on his nose, Max saw the drone's weak spot highlighted in red. He raised the **SNOTSHOOTER** to his shoulder.

He held his breath.

And then, he fired.

CHAPTER THREE

TANKS A LOT

A shiny, sticky ball of concentrated snot shot from the end of the cane. It made a high-pitched whistling sound as it streaked through the air.

BADOING!

The snot-bullet struck a direct hit on the reset button, and the drone spun out of control. It clattered against the side of the Bogey Bus, then bounced with a **THUD** off the back of Gunk's head.

'**OW!**' he yelped, rolling upright and running for cover just as the other Goozillas let out a cheer.

'**YOU DID IT, MAX!**' cried Gloop.

'I knew you would!' said Captain Crust.

'Can I get my glasses back?' asked Joe, bumping blindly into the Bogey Bus.

Max smiled as he handed Joe and Captain Crust their items back. He remembered the day he'd bought both the Gadget Glasses and **SNOTSHOOTER** cane in the app, but had never dreamed he'd get a chance to use them himself. Between them, they'd cost Max hundreds of his hard-earned Dung Dollars, but it was definitely money well spent!

'OK, we stopped the drone, so let's go and get the **GLOB** piece back,' Max cried. The Goozillas all shuffled uncomfortably . . . except Big Blob, who just stared blankly at the ground.

'If only it were that simple,' said Captain Crust. He checked for danger, then led the rest of the group out from behind the Bogey Bus. 'The **GLOB** piece is in there.'

The captain pointed along the long, narrow street where a mushroom stood at the far end, surrounded on all sides by **BARBED WIRE**. The mushroom was dark green with patches of black and brown sticking to it like **MOULD**.

'Is that what I think it is?' asked Max.

'Depends,' said Joe. 'Do you think it's a giant monkey's bum?'

Max frowned. 'Er . . . no.'

'Good,' Joe grinned. 'Because it isn't one of them.'

'It's the **FUNGUS FORT**,' said Gloop, lowering his voice to a whisper. 'A high-security fortress surrounded by **BOOBY TRAPS** and state-of-the-art **DEFENCES**.'

Max groaned. 'And don't tell me—Bubble Kitten is in there?'

'Yep,' said Atishoo from the top of Captain Crust's hat. 'She's managed to sneak in and activate the defences. No one has ever been able to get past those before.'

'**UNTIL TODAY!**' said Gunk, twirling his gun on one slimy finger. 'I'm going

31

to storm that place and blast a hole right through it. Who's with me?'

Captain Crust sighed. 'When will you learn, Gunk? Warfare isn't about rushing in with all guns blazing. It's about strategy. It's about planning.'

'**BORING!**' Gunk sighed. 'I'm a shoot first, ask questions later kind of guy.'

'More like a jump first, land flat on his face later kind of guy,' Joe quipped. Max and Gloop both snorted with laughter, but quickly stopped when Gunk turned and glared at them.

'What's that noise?' asked Big Blob. Everyone looked up at him in surprise.

'What noise?' asked Max, but then he heard it too. It was a low rumbling, a bit like

the sound the Bogey Bus made when it
was rolling over rough ground.

Max and the others turned to see
a tiny tank trundling towards them. It
was about the size of a supermarket
shopping trolley, but much closer to the
ground, and it was closing in on them
. . . **QUICKLY**!

'**ATTACK!**' Gunk roared, but
Captain Crust held up his cane,
blocking Gunk's path.

'Not so fast,' the captain said.
'Look. It has no gun turret.'

Sure enough, where the gun should have
been, there was a metal pole sticking straight
up in the air. A television teetered on the top.
The screen was black, but as the tank drew

closer, an image
flickered into life.

'ATTENTION,
GOO-LOSERS!'

purred an all-too-
familiar voice.

On the screen,
the pink-furred Bubble
Kitten narrowed her big green eyes and
wrinkled her heart-shaped nose into a sneer.
'Oh, and I see Meddling Max is with you too.
What an unpleasant surprise.'

Joe squinted at the screen. 'Hey, Bubble
Kitten. Is that a bogey on your face?'

'UGH! WHAT? WHERE?'

the cat spluttered. She spat on
her paws and frantically scrubbed
her fur. It wasn't until Joe, Max,
and Gloop all fell about laughing
that she realized she'd been tricked.
'That wasn't funny.'

'It was pretty funny!' called a voice
from somewhere behind Bubble Kitten.
Max recognized it as Sugar Paws Puppy,
the evil kitty's clueless sidekick. A bright
blue paw reached into view and waved
enthusiastically. 'Hello everyone!'

Bubble Kitten slapped the paw away,
then rolled her eyes. 'Give me strength,'
she muttered, then she tried her best
to look wicked and sinister again.

'Anyway, fun as it is to catch up with you all, I wanted to let you know that there's no way you're getting the **GOLDEN GLOB** piece this time. It's safely locked up in this giant mushroom with me. Even if you could get past my defences, you'd never break through the walls.'

'Don't bet on it,' said Max. 'We've beaten you before.'

'Yes,' Bubble Kitten smirked. 'But this time, I've brought a friend.'

Gunk snorted. 'Sugar Paws? He's not exactly a threat.'

'**NO, NOT THAT OAF,**' Bubble Kitten said, and she raised her paws above her head.

'BEHOLD, THE GREATEST WARRIOR OF ALL TIME. THE ONE . . . THE ONLY . . . SCAMPY HAMSTER!'

Nothing happened. Max and the Goozillas looked at each other and shrugged. On screen, Bubble Kitten tutted. 'Sugar Paws! The button. Press the button. Seriously, do I have to do everything my—'

The rest of Bubble Kitten's sentence was cut off as the screen changed to show a row of wooden dummies in the shape of the Goozillas.

'Wait, is that supposed to be us?' asked Gloop, but before anyone could answer, a purple blur **STREAKED** across the screen.

There were a few screamed '**Hi-ya!**' and a lot of cracking. By the time the blur passed, the dummy Goozillas were nothing more than scraps of broken wood.

'I hope not,' gulped Gloop.

The view changed to show a short, stocky creature with purple fur and a fiery-red headband.

'Is that a hamster?' Max wondered, peering at the screen.

'Hiiiii-ya!' yelped the creature, unleashing a volley of kicks and punches that made Max and the Goozillas jump back in fright.

'SCAMPY HAMSTER,

WORLD'S GREATEST WARRIOR!

YA!'

'You don't look so tough,' said Gunk.

On screen, Scampy picked up a stone slab and smashed it with his forehead. It crumbled to dust and drifted to the ground.

'Easy,' said Gunk, bending and picking up a stone. 'Watch this.'

He **SLAMMED** the rock against his head. It made a loud **SPLAT** and Gunk's head suddenly became very flat. A moment later, he fell over.

'Impressive,' sniggered Bubble Kitten, as her face replaced Scampy on the screen. 'But perhaps you see the truth now, Goo-losers. I've got the **GOLDEN GLOB** piece, and with Scampy Hamster at my side, there is no way you're ever getting your hands on it!'

CHAPTER FOUR

TOWERS OF TERROR

Bubble Kitten's cackle echoed from the TV's speakers. '**YOU FOOLS!**' she laughed. 'You pathetic, snivelling, **slime**-coated—'

Big Blob brought his fist down on the tank, **CRUSHING** it. Bubble Kitten's laugh became a high-pitched whine, then the screen sparked, fizzled, and died completely.

'Thanks, Blob,' said Max. He bent over the unconscious Gunk and slapped him in the face a few times. 'Gunk. Wake up.'

'Warugh?' Gunk yelped, flicking open his eyes. He looked around. 'What hit me?'

'You did,' said Joe.

'With a big rock,' added Gloop.

'It was pretty funny,' giggled Atishoo.

Captain Crust tucked his cane under his arm and sucked on his moustache. 'Well, what isn't funny is that blasted cat!' he said. 'If she has the **GLOB** piece in **FUNGUS FORT**, getting it is going to be very difficult indeed.'

'I say we charge straight for it,' said Gunk, leaping to his feet. Or to the wobbly bits where his feet should be, at least.

'Yes, well you would say that,' said Captain Crust. 'But I'd hardly call that sound military strategy.'

Max stepped away from the others and peered towards **FUNGUS FORT**. Although he didn't play this level often, he got the feeling that something was missing. Something important.

Behind him, the Goozillas argued about what to do. Joe suggested taking the Bogey Bus, but Gloop pointed out that the mucus tank had been damaged in the drone attack, and all the bus's fuel had leaked out.

Captain Crust suggested trying a sneak attack, but the barbed wire barricades ran all the way around the big mushroom fortress, and there was no other way in.

'THEN A DIRECT ATTACK IT IS!'

roared Gunk.

'LET'S DO THIS. CHAAAAAAARGE!'

Holding his gun in the air, Gunk shot past Max and raced along the street.

'Come back, you reckless fool!' cried Captain Crust, but Gunk ignored him.

Max felt the ground beneath his feet rumble. He looked down and frowned for a moment. Was it an earthquake? Was the volcano about to erupt?

And then he remembered. He remembered what was missing!

'**GUNK, LOOK OUT!**' he shouted, just as the whole street began to shudder and shake. Six wide towers rose from below the ground, **SHATTERING** the tarmac as they grew up and up and up towards the sky.

At the top of each tower was an **ENORMOUS** cannon. All six of them

47

rotated and took aim at Gunk, who stood on the ground far below, his mouth hanging open.

'Ooh, this isn't good,' Gunk had time to mutter, before the cannons opened fire. Colourful laser blasts rained down around Gunk as he **DODGED**, **DARTED**, **ZIGGED**, **ZAGGED**, and generally ran for his life.

The ground erupted beside him, throwing up clouds of dust and spraying him with shards of hot stone that made his **slime** sizzle.

A final laser blast hit the ground directly behind him. The tarmac exploded, launching Gunk high into the air. Max and the Goozillas watched as Gunk sailed upwards, flipping over and over, then plummeted back to the ground.

KERSPLOOT!

'**OW**,' Gunk grunted. He peeled his face off the pavement and flopped onto his back. 'Look out,' he wheezed. 'They've got gun towers.'

'Really? You don't say,' said Captain Crust.

The group was out of the towers' range, so they were safe for the moment. But if they wanted to get the **GLOB** piece, they had to find a way past those cannons somehow.

The lenses of Joe's Gadget Glasses turned red as he scanned the towers. 'Do you want the good news or the bad news?' he asked. 'And, just so no one gets disappointed in a minute, I may as well tell you now—there

50

is no good news.'

Max sighed. 'We should probably hear the bad news, then.'

'OK, Bad News Number One: those towers have been upgraded to the highest level. One direct hit from their lasers, and we're done for.'

The other Goozillas groaned.

'And Bad News Number Two: I don't see any weaknesses. Those things are indestructible.'

'They're not quite indestructible,' said Max. 'If I remember rightly, in the game you can unlock a tank with a **GIANT** laser turret. It can **BLAST** the towers to bits.'

'Great!' cheered Captain Crust. 'And do you have a tank with a giant laser turret?'

Max blushed slightly. 'Uh, no. No. Sorry.'

'Oh,' said Captain Crust, deflating.
'Right.'

Gloop straightened up suddenly. 'Wait! We don't have a tank, but we do have laser turrets.'

'What? Where?' asked Joe, looking around.

'Gloop's right!' said Max. He pointed to the towers, and to the turrets mounted on top of them. 'One, two, three, four, five, six!'

'I'm afraid you've got it wrong,' said Captain Crust. 'Those aren't our laser turrets, they're under the control of Bubble Kitten.'

Max spun on the spot until he was facing Captain Crust's hat. 'That doesn't mean we can't use them! Atishoo, your **sneezes** can launch you through the air, right?'

Atishoo nodded. Because he had no head, this meant he just sort of bobbed up and down. 'Sure can! Why?'

Max picked the little Goozilla up and sat him on his shoulder. 'I was wondering—just how far and how

FAST

do you think you can fly?'

CHAPTER FIVE

MOVING TARGET

Big Blob stood in the middle of the road, tossing Atishoo from hand to hand.

'**HEY, C-C-CAREFUL!**' the smallest Goozilla protested. Big Blob stopped throwing him around and balanced him on his palm, instead.

'Sorry, Atishoo. I thought you were a ball.'

'OK, are you both ready to do this?' asked Max. He was standing beside Big Blob, while the rest of the Goozillas hung back, safely out of harm's way.

'**READY!**' chirped Atishoo.

There was a long pause.

'Ready,' said Big Blob, at last.

Max patted the giant Goozilla on the back. 'Just remember, as high as you can. Atishoo, be careful.'

'Come on, I'll be fine!' Atishoo said, but he couldn't hide the tremble in his voice.

Max looked up at the towers. The plan was risky, he knew. Crazy, even. It needed split-second timing and precision aiming, or it would all go terribly wrong. If there was any other way of getting past the towers, Max would have taken it, but this was the only chance they had. The fate of the **WORLD OF SLIME** rested on the next few moments.

'OK, then, Blob. **THROW!**'

It took a few seconds for Max's command to reach Big Blob's brain. When it did, Blob drew back his arm like a baseball pitcher and took aim at the stone ceiling a long way overhead.

'**HERE GOES!**' Atishoo yelped, and then—

FOOOOoOM!

—Big Blob *LAUNCHED* him upwards at **BLINDING** speed.

Max watched the little blob
become even smaller as he
climbed higher and higher.
'Not yet, not yet . . .' he
whispered, then:
'NOW, ATISHOO!'

On cue, Atishoo let rip with a **Sneeze** so loud it rolled like **THUNDER** inside the vast cavern. The force of the **Sneeze** launched him along the street, *FASTER* than a *SPEEDING* bullet.

All six of the tower turrets whirred as they took aim. The first two towers *FIRED* at exactly the same time, but Atishoo was moving too fast. The laser fire scorched the air as it criss-crossed behind him.

Each blast struck the gun opposite, and they both **EXPLODED** in a shower of sparks.

'It's working!' Max cried. 'It's working!'

Towers three and four tried to track the **SPEEDING** Atishoo, but he was too small, and too **FAST**, and those gun turrets were blasted to pieces, too.

The momentum from Atishoo's **sneeze** was wearing off. He slowed down as he sailed past the final set of turrets. They turned quickly. Their barrels flashed red and two streaks of laser-fire tore through the air, heading

straight
for the helpless
little
Goozilla.

'**YIKES!**' Atishoo yelped. He rolled himself into a ball and *PLUNGED* towards the ground. The blasts passed through the spot where he had just been. Then, with a **BA-BOOM**, both guns exploded.

Atishoo hit the ground, bounced twice, then rolled to a stop just millimetres from the sharp points of a barbed wire barricade. He lay there for a moment, catching his breath, then rolled backwards to safety.

Max raced down the street to where Atishoo had landed, and snatched him up. 'You did it!' he cheered.

'Hey, all I did was **sneeze**,' said Atishoo. 'You came up with the plan.'

'You were both awesome!' said Joe, as he, Gloop, and Gunk ran over to join them. Captain Crust hobbled along behind, smiling broadly beneath his moustache. Big Blob trailed at the back, gazing up at the towers in wonder.

'Do you see, Gunk?' wheezed Captain Crust. 'Do you see the advantages of strategy and planning?'

'Yeah, yeah. Whatever you say, bub,' said Gunk. He raised his gun above his head. 'Now come on, we need to get through this barbed wire. **CHAAAAAARGE!**'

Captain Crust sighed as Gunk raced straight towards the spiky barricades. 'Seriously,' the old Goozilla muttered. 'Will he ever learn?'

CHAPTER SIX

ANGRY BLOBS

It took several minutes to free Gunk from the barbed wire. He'd tried to climb over the first barricade, but had immediately got himself stuck on the spikes. It took all the other Goozillas, working together, to release him.

They had heaved and stretched him until he finally twanged free with a gloopy **SQUELCH** and a rubbery boing! Once he was untangled, Gunk flopped down onto the ground. 'Maybe you should all go on without me,' he said, glumly.

'What? Why would we do that?' asked Max.

Gunk shrugged. 'Well, I mean, I'm useless, aren't I? The captain's right. I rush in without thinking. I'm no help. I'm just another problem for you to deal with.'

'I don't recall ever saying that,' said Captain Crust. 'Granted, you're a little quick off the mark sometimes, but—'

'It's true, though,' said Gunk, standing up. 'I'll only get in the way. Go on without me. I'll be in the bus.'

'**GUNK, WAIT!**' Gloop called after him, but Gunk just trudged sadly past and slithered his way back towards the Bogey Bus.

'HI\|\|-YA!'

The other Goozillas and Max turned
to see Scampy Hamster land a perfect
SOMERSAULT on the other side of
the barbed wire barricades. He had two
sticks in his hand, connected
together by a length of chain.
He flailed them around until
they became just a blur of speed.

'Aw, your little friend has run
away like a coward!' Scampy sneered.
'**HOW PATHETIC! YA!**'

He jumped into a flying **SPINNING**
kick, then landed expertly on the exact same
spot. 'Though I think he may be the wisest
of you all. There is no way through. You are
defeated. You have lost! **HIII-YA!**'

'Oh yeah? We'll see about that!' said Max.

'BRING IT ON! YOU WANT SOME OF THIS?'

screeched Scampy.

He flipped, spun, punched the air several times very quickly, then kicked four times at head height without once lowering his leg.

It was all very impressive. 'Don't make me come over there!'

'Ha! As if you could,' said Captain Crust.

Screaming, '**Hiyaaaaaaa!**' Scampy Hamster **SOMERSAULTED** over the barbed wire fences. He landed directly in front of the captain, pulled off an impressive jumping **KICK**, and knocked the old Goozilla's hat off. The hat, and Atishoo, both **SPRAWLED** on the ground.

Stunned, the Goozillas could only watch as Scampy demonstrated his acrobatic skills once again by **FLIPPING** and **SOMERSAULTING** back the way he'd come.

Tucking his weapons into his headband, Scampy **BACKFLIPPED** several times until he was right by the wall of the **FUNGUS FORT**. A rope lowered from the top of the wall and he quickly scrambled up it. 'That was just a warning shot, losers!' Scampy called, before he **FLIPPED** over the top of the wall and vanished back into the fort.

'Where does Bubble Kitten find these idiots?' Gloop wondered.

'Idiot or not, he's right,' said Captain Crust, **GROANING** as he stooped to pick up his hat and Atishoo. 'Look at all those barricades. There's no way we can get past them all.'

'Can we dig under them?' asked Joe.

'I'm afraid not,' said the captain. 'If we dig, we'll simply end up in the level below.

I've had quite enough of mazes for one lifetime.'

'If we can't go under, how about over?' Gloop suggested.

'Big Blob could throw us all,' said Atishoo. 'It's not that bad once you get past the being more **TERRIFIED** than you've ever been in your life part.'

'I fear throwing us that far is beyond even Blob's strength,' said Captain Crust.

Max was only half-listening. He studied the barbed wire, then looked up at the smoking laser-turret towers standing on either side.

'Do you know something? I don't always play **WORLD OF SLIME**,' Max announced.

The Goozillas looked at him in surprise. 'Uh . . . OK,' said Gloop. 'We won't take it personally.'

'No, I mean . . . there's another game I play sometimes, too. It's got these birds, and . . .' Max's voice trailed off and he shrugged. 'Do you know what? It'll be easier if I just show you.'

A few minutes later, Max held tightly to Gloop and braced himself.

At least, he thought it was Gloop. On Max's instructions, the Goozillas—minus Gunk, who was now back at the Bogey Bus—had all linked arms and stretched themselves between the two towers like an

ENORMOUS rubber band. Captain Crust wasn't as stretchy as he used to be, so Max could recognize him, but the others were stretched so THIN he could barely tell where one Goozilla ended and another began.

Max gritted his teeth and pushed back with his legs, stretching the Goozillas even further. 'Almost . . . there . . .' he groaned.

'You can do it, Max!' said Captain Crust.

The rubbery band of Goozillas was as stretched out as it could possibly go.

'OK, RELEASING IN THREE . . . TWO . . . ONE!'

Max raised his legs. The Goozillas snapped forwards and upwards like the elastic of a slingshot. Max **SCREAMED**. The Goozillas **SCREAMED**. Even the wind seemed to **SCREAM** as they were catapulted through the air.

'Oof!' Max thudded against the wall of the *FUNGUS FORT*, then slid to the ground.

'Really should have thought that through a bit more,' he groaned.

A rain of **SPLATS** and **SPLOOTS** fell around him as the Goozillas all landed, one after the other, then twanged back into their normal shapes.

'WE MADE IT!'

said Max, not quite believing his plan had worked. He rubbed his head where he had smacked against the wall. 'I mean, I should have got one of you to cushion my landing, but we made it. We're over the barbed wire!'

'AND RIGHT INTO MY TRAP!'

announced a voice from the top of the wall. The Goozillas and Max looked up to see Scampy Hamster and Bubble Kitten both leaning over the wall. Bubble Kitten smiled, flashing her sharp teeth. 'Scampy, release the hamster balls!'

'OF DOOM!' added Sugar Paws Puppy, appearing at the top of the wall beside the others.

Bubble Kitten sighed. 'No, not "of Doom".

. . Oh, forget it. Just release the balls.'

'HIIII-YA!'

shrieked Scampy, ducking out of sight.

From inside the fort there came a low **RUMBLING** sound. Several small doors mounted high in the walls opened, and dozens of plastic balls rolled out. The balls were around half the size of a football, and inside each one was a tiny purple hamster in a red headband.

The balls dropped to the ground and rolled into position so they completely surrounded the Goozillas.

'Uh-oh,' said Gloop. 'I have a bad feeling about this.'

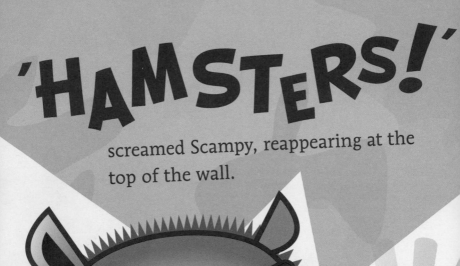

'HAMSTERS!'

screamed Scampy, reappearing at the top of the wall.

CHAPTER SEVEN

HAVING A BALL

Max yelped in fright as a hamster ball launched itself into the air and rocketed towards his face. He ducked, only to hear an '**OOYAH!**' from behind him as the ball thonked Gloop between the eyes.

'**STAY CLOSE TOGETHER!**' Captain Crust barked. 'They can't get us if we stick close to one another like—'

A hamster ball hit him on the back of the head, knocking his hat off. '**OW! I SAY!**' he protested, before another of the balls slammed into his tummy doubling him over.

Max swung a kick at one of the approaching balls, but it swerved suddenly and he lost his balance. As he fell, Max heard the hamster inside the ball giggling with glee.

It looked more or less exactly like Scampy, but much smaller. This one was actually hamster-sized, whereas Scampy looked to be almost as tall as Max himself.

Hitting the ground, Max immediately tried to scramble to his feet, but another hamster ball knocked his legs from beneath him and he crashed down again. The other Goozillas were falling, too. Joe and Gloop both hit the ground at the

same time, while Big Blob
struggled under the weight
of dozens of the balls, which *HURLED*
themselves at him from every
direction at once.

'Oh, how pathetic!' shouted
Bubble Kitten from high on the
wall. 'I can't even bring myself to
look.

TAKE CARE, GOO-LOSERS.'

Max tried to crawl to safety, but several
hamster balls rolled up onto his back,
holding him down.

'TIIM

the little critters cheered,
as Big Blob lost his balance and
toppled like a great oak tree.

Atishoo peeped out from beneath Captain Crust's hat, then gasped when a hamster ball landed on the old man's back, **PINNING** him to the ground.

'B-blast it,' wheezed Captain Crust. 'We were so close!'

Max lay on his front, struggling against the weight of the creatures on his back. He stopped wriggling and watched as one of the balls slowly rolled towards him. Inside, the hamster chittered wickedly. Its beady little eyes burned red as its mouth pulled into a nasty smirk.

'S-stay away!' Max said. 'I'm warning you.'

'We can do what we like,' the hamster hissed. '**AND THERE'S NOTHING YOU CAN DO TO STOP US!**'

'GERONIMO!'

'Huh?' said the hamster, then a ball of high-speed goo **SHATTERED** the plastic ball to pieces and coated the rodent from head to toe in thick, gloopy slime. The slime plastered the hamster to the ground like glue, stopping it in its tracks.

SPUT! SPUT! SPUT!

Morc goo-blasts *STREAKED* down from the sky. More hamster balls exploded. With a roar of effort, Max rolled over, just in time to see Gunk come swooping down from above. He had his *SLUDGESPUTTER* in one hand, and was firing round after round of sticky green blobs at the panicking hamsters.

89

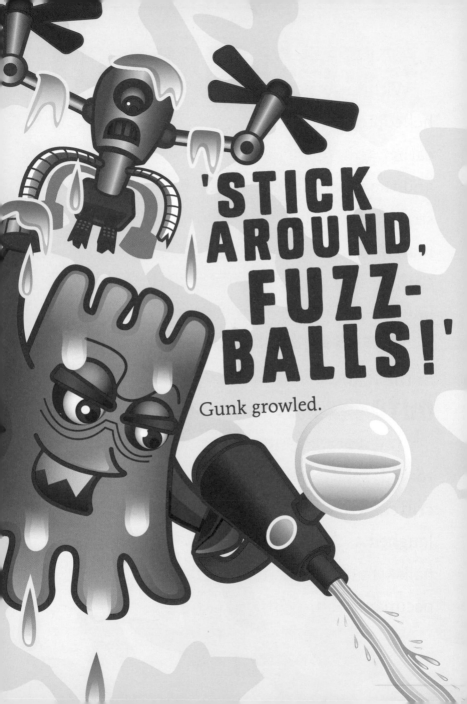

With his other hand, he held onto the helicopter drone that Max had shot down earlier. It had been quite clumsily repaired, and the rotor blades whined as they struggled with Gunk's weight, but it had managed to carry him over the barricades. Gunk released his grip, *SPINNING* aroundand *FIRING* as he fell.

'**RETREAT!**' squeaked one of the hamsters. '**WE'RE OUTGUNNED**.'

'You'd better believe it, bub!' Gunk roared, splatting down behind the fleeing critters. Gunk threw back his head and laughed as he rained **slime** on the other balls, shattering them and sticking the occupants to the ground.

When every one of the balls had been trapped or destroyed, Gunk spun his **SLUDGESPUTTER** like a cowboy, then blew down the barrel. 'Well, well. Maybe I'm not so useless, after all!'

'That was amazing!' cried Max. Gloop and Joe jumped up and trapped Gunk in a squidgy hug.

'You saved us!' Joe cried.

'Get off!' grunted Gunk, although he didn't put up much of a fight.

'Excellent work, Gunk! Jolly good show!' said Captain Crust, pulling his hat back on. 'Perhaps we'll get to the **GLOB** piece yet!'

'**OR PERHAPS YOU WON'T!**' bellowed Bubble Kitten. '**LAUNCH THE MUCUS MISSILE!**'

'LAUNCH THE MUCUS MISSILE!'

screeched Scampy Hamster.

He was standing right next to Bubble Kitten at the top of the fort, and his sudden scream almost made her jump out of her fur.

'**OF DOOOOOOM!**' called a voice from inside. Bubble Kitten rolled her eyes and shook her head.

'Why must I be surrounded by idiots?'
she sighed, then she ducked as a bright
red rocket roared up out of the fort, pulled
a loop-the-loop in the air, then hurtled
towards the Goozillas on the ground below.

'What do we do?' gasped Gloop.

'Get blown to bits, probably,' Joe guessed.

'Do you trust me?' demanded Gunk.

The others blinked. 'What?' said Captain
Crust. 'Uh . . . yes. Yes. We trust you.'

Gunk raised his gun above his head and
pointed to the wall of *FUNGUS FORT*. 'Then

CHAAAAAARGE!'

CHAPTER EIGHT

STORMING THE FORT

The Goozillas and Max *RACED* towards the wall, the Mucus Missile screaming after them.

'You blasted fool!' panted Captain Crust. 'I should never have trusted you. There's nowhere left to run!'

'Well spotted,' cried Gunk over his shoulder. 'Everyone **DOWN!**'

Frantically, everyone dived to the ground. Max felt the heat of the Mucus Missile as it roared above them. Then the whole cavern was filled with a sound like thunder. And then it was filled with a sound like a giant **sneeze**.

Dust and smoke rolled over them, making

Max cough and choke. He heaved himself to his feet just as the smoke began to clear.

'Gunk, I never thought I'd say this, but you're a genius!' said Joe.

There, right in front of them, was a big round hole in the wall of **FUNGUS FORT**. And beyond it, just past a pile of rubble, the broken bits of Mucus Missile, and the biggest pile of gloopy green snot Max had ever seen, was the **GOLDEN GLOB** piece.

'Grab it, quick!' Captain Crust barked.

Max, Gloop, Joe, and Gunk all raced for the **GLOB** piece together. It was almost within their grasp when a purple streak slammed onto the ground right ahead of them, shattering the concrete floor into a spider's web pattern.

'Yaaaaaa!' screeched Scampy Hamster. His hands sliced the air in a flurry of punches and chops, then he lowered into a fighting stance and bared his sharp hamster teeth. 'You want the **GLOB** piece? First, you must get through me!'

Captain Crust, Atishoo, and Big Blob all clambered through the hole in the wall, but stopped when they saw the hamster.

Scampy pulled his **DEADLY** nunchucks from his headband and flailed them expertly. Max and the others watched them **SWING** and **PIVOT**, **TWIRL** and **SPIN**, their eyes following every blurred move.

Behind Scampy, Bubble Kitten dropped

silently to the floor.

'**AAAAAAAAAAAAAHHH!**'

Sugar Paws hit the ground, face-first beside his master.

'I'm OK,' he said, his voice muffled by the ground. 'Totally meant to do that.'

'Congratulations on making it this far,' Bubble Kitten purred. 'You've done much better than I expected. But now it's the end of the line. You can't possibly defeat Scampy. He's the **GREATEST WARRIOR WHO EVER LIVED**.'

To prove the cat's point, Scampy **SOMERSAULTED** twice, twirled into a **SPINNING** tornado kick, then **SPUN** his weapons until they looked like a solid circle of metal and wood.

'Greatest warrior who ever lived,' Gunk growled. 'Meet the greatest gun that ever existed.'

He took aim at the hamster and pulled the trigger. The **SLUDGESPUTTER** let out a sad sort of farting noise, and a trickle of goo dribbled from the end. 'Uh-oh,' Gunk groaned. 'Out of ammo.'

'HI!'

Scampy Hamster launched himself at
Gunk, arms and legs kicking and slashing
and chopping at the air. Instinctively, Gunk
brought his head forward to duck.

There was a **THONK** as Scampy's nose hit the top of Gunk's head, then the hamster **STAGGERED** back, his wide eyes filling with tears.

'**HEY! H-HE HIT ME!**' Scampy yelped.

'He hit me right in the face with his head.'

'What?' Gunk frowned. 'No I didn't! You hit me right on my head with your face!'

'He did! He hit me right on the nose!' Scampy said, his bottom lip **WOBBLING**. 'That really hurt.'

Bubble Kitten's jaw dropped. 'So? Who cares? What are you talking about? **ATTACK!**'

'No way!' Scampy sobbed. 'They hit back!

You didn't tell me they hit back. I'm not playing anymore.'

'**PLAYING?!**' Bubble Kitten yelped. 'What do you mean? You're supposed to be the **GREATEST WARRIOR IN THE WORLD**. You said your fighting skills were legendary.'

'They are!' said Scampy. 'But I've never had to actually use them before. It's not fair if they hit back!' He **TILTED** his head back and pointed to his nose. 'Is it bleeding? I bet it's bleeding, isn't it? **IT'S NOT FAIR!**'

To everyone's amazement, the hamster burst into tears. 'You're a big bully!' he howled, as he ran past Gunk, out through the hole in the fort's wall, and off along the street.

'Well,' said Joe, once Scampy was out of sight. 'I did not see that coming.'

Everyone turned to Bubble Kitten. She smiled nervously and backed away. 'Guys. Come on. Let's talk about this,' she said. 'This has all just been a misunderstanding. Right? We'll all laugh about it later.'

Gunk picked up the fragment of **GOLDEN GLOB** and turned to Captain Crust. 'May I?'

'Be my guest, dear boy,' said the captain.

Gunk pressed the **GLOB** piece against his slimy belly, then shoved it inside. A golden light **SHIMMERED** inside him for a moment, and he seemed to grow a few centimetres before everyone's eyes.

Bubble Kitten grabbed Sugar Paws by the scruff of his neck and hoisted him to his feet. 'You might have the **GLOB** piece, but there are still three more out there, and I only need one to stop you bringing back the **slime**. So long, Goo-Losers!' she sneered, then she quickly blew a bubble shield around her and her sidekick, protecting them from harm.

Captain Crust cleared his throat. 'I say, Gunk. How about you show us that "rushing in" tactic of yours once more? For old time's sake.'

Gunk grinned. 'You got it, bub,' he said, then he lowered his shoulder, took aim at the bubble, and charged!

The powered-up Gunk slammed into the shimmering sphere. Inside, Bubble Kitten and Sugar Paws both screamed as they rocketed across the **FUNGUS FORT**.

'W-W-WE'LL G-G-G-GET YOU F-F-F-FOR THIS!'

Bubble Kitten cried,

as she bounced around inside the bubble. Then, with a **CRASH**, the bubble **SMASHED** through the wall of the **FUNGUS FORT**, sending the Sicklies hurtling back towards the World of Pets.

And just in the nick of time, too!

BEEP-BEEP-BEEP!

'Oh no! It's my screen time alarm,' Max groaned. 'I'm about to get locked out.'

'See you soon, Max!' said Gloop.

'Catch you later!' replied Max.

Captain Crust and Gunk both saluted, and Max thought he heard Atishoo say something, too, but it was too faint to make it out as the world began to **TUMBLE** and **SPIN** around him.

CHAPTER NINE

ADVENTURE'S END

'Muuuum! He's not here!'

Max flipped his covers down and sat up in bed. Over by his door, his little sister, Amy, screamed in fright.

'Amy! It's just me!' he said, trying to calm her down.

Amy stopped screaming, but continued to stare at him as if he were a ghost. 'Where did you come from?' she asked.

'I was under my covers. Er . . . hiding,' said Max.

'No you weren't,' said Amy, her eyes narrowing. 'I looked.'

Max shrugged. 'No, you're right. A magic **sneeze** transported me into the **WORLD OF SLIME**, and I was having an adventure with the Goozillas.'

Amy scowled. 'Stop being silly,' she replied. She held out her hands. 'Mum said I can have the tablet.'

Max looked at the screen as the timer counted down the last few seconds. On screen, the Goozillas all waved up at him, then the app closed itself and a little padlock symbol appeared in the corner of the icon. There would be no getting back to **WORLD OF SLIME** until tomorrow.

'Fine, you can have it,' Max said, passing the device to his sister. She snatched it eagerly and immediately tapped on the

114

cutesy pink World of Pets icon.

Amy was halfway out of the room when she let out a **GASP** of shock. 'What's happened to Bubble Kitten?' she yelped, showing Max the tablet. On screen, Bubble Kitten and Sugar Paws Puppy both had little circles spinning around their heads. Both of them looked a little green in the face, like they were about to throw up at any moment.

'Ooh, yeah,' said Max. 'They look like they've been in a fight.'

Amy's face lit up. 'I know what will cheer them up. Their green faces will be perfect for testing out the new make-up I bought for them!'

She skipped out of the room. Max waited until she was downstairs before letting out the laugh he'd been holding in. He'd seen Amy's make-up skills in action, and almost felt sorry for Bubble Kitten.

Almost, but not quite.

Three **GOLDEN GLOB** pieces had been collected, but there were still three more to go. Bubble Kitten wouldn't stop trying to take over the **WORLD OF SLIME**, but that was OK—because Max would never stop trying to protect it!

Join Max and **THE GOOZILLAS** on their next adventure in the

WORLD OF SLIME...

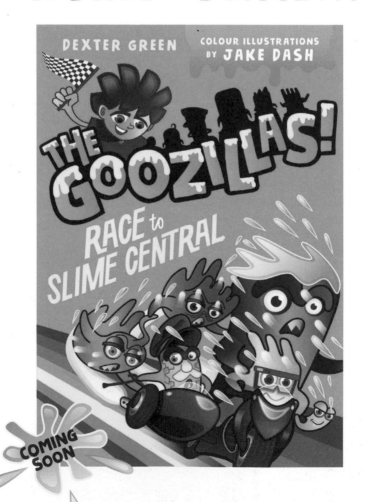